THE AMAZING ADVENTURES OF SUPERMAN!

Creatures from Planet X!

by Yale Stewart

Superman created by Jerry Siegel and Joe Shuster
by special arrangement with the Jerry Siegel family

Paintree is an imprint of Capstone Global Library Limited, a company incorporated in England and Wales having its registered office at 264 Banbury Road, Oxford, OX2 7DY – Registered company number: 6695582

www.raintree.co.uk
myorders@raintree.co.uk

STAR37090

ISBN 978 1 47472 915 4
20 19 18 17 16
10 9 8 7 6 5 4 3 2 1

A CIP catalogue for this book is available from the British Library.

Editor: Donald Lemke
Designer: Bob Lentz

Printed and bound in China

CONTENTS

Born among the stars.
Raised on planet Earth.
With incredible powers,
he became the
World's Greatest Super Hero.
These are...

Chapter 1

AIR SHOW

Reporter Clark Kent looks up at the sky. "A perfect day for an air show," he says.

A dozen jets soar high above him, performing tricks. The crowd cheers.

Suddenly, one jet begins

to rock, shake and smoke.

"What's happening?" says

the pilot, Hal Jordan.

Hal looks outside his jet.

He can't believe his eyes...

Hundreds of glowing

yellow insects attack the jet!

They tear apart its wings.

The jet begins to fall.

On the ground, the crowd runs and hides. Clark Kent doesn't move.

"This looks like a job for Superman!" says Clark. He takes off his glasses and shirt. A uniform is beneath.

"I must save that pilot!"

Superman says. WHOOSH!

He soars into the sky.

BOOM! The jet explodes in

a flash of green light.

"Green Lantern!" says Superman. He greets his super hero friend.

"The one and only," replies Hal Jordan, wearing his green power ring.

"What planet did these creatures come from?" asks Superman. "I've never seen anything glow that colour."

Green Lantern stares at

the yellow insects. "I have."

He tightens his fist. "This is

the work of Sinestro!"

Chapter 2

RING OF FEAR

In the city of Metropolis, Sinestro stands on top of the Daily Planet Building. He creates thousands of insects with his yellow ring. "My plan is working!" he shouts.

Sinestro's
insects swarm
the streets below.
People scream
in fear.

"Their fear is
giving me power,"
he says, laughing.
"Soon, I'll be strong
enough to take
over the city!"

The super heroes arrive

at the Daily Planet Building.

"Great plan, Sinestro,"

says Green Lantern.

"But I hope you planned

on us," adds Superman.

With super-speed, the
hero flies at Sinestro. The
villain creates a giant insect
shield with his power ring.

THUD! The shield stops
Superman in midair.

"I can't hit him!" says
the Man of Steel.

"His ring is powered by fear," Hal replies. He points his own ring at the shield. "But there's something even more powerful…"

Chapter 3

TEAMWORK!

"Green Lantern's light!"

Green Lantern shouts.

With his ring, the hero

can create anything he can

imagine. A jackhammer

appears in the sky.

WHAM! WHAM!

Green Lantern hammers

at Sinestro's shield. The

glowing, yellow insects

won't crack or chip.

"Time to break out the

big gun!" Hal jokes.

Green Lantern creates a
giant cannon with his ring.
KA-BLAMO! He blasts
the shield with cannonballs.

The shield of insects does not break. In fact, it grows twice as large! "Give up!" Sinestro shouts. "Your weapons are useless."

Superman turns to Green Lantern. "Maybe it's not the weapons," says the hero. "Maybe it's the ammo."

Green Lantern smiles. "Get in," he replies.

Superman climbs inside Green Lantern's cannon. He straightens out his body like a missile.

"Ready..." he says.

"Aim..." adds Hal.

"FIRE!" the heroes shout. In a blinding flash, Superman explodes from the cannon. He strikes the shield with his fists.

CRASSSH! This time, the

shield shatters. The insects

crumble into powder and

disappear.

"NO!" cries Sinestro.

Green Lantern traps the super-villain inside a cage of green energy.

"One thing is definitely more powerful than fear," says Superman.

"What's that?" asks Hal.

"Teamwork," replies the Man of Steel, waving goodbye to his friend. "Thanks for the amazing adventure!"

SUPERMAN'S
SECRET MESSAGE!

Hey, kids! What's a super hero's greatest power?

Use the code below to solve the secret message!

air show event where pilots show their skills to fly aircraft in unusual and exciting ways

crumble break into small pieces

imagine picture something in your mind

jackhammer machine used to drill hard materials

swarm group of insects that gather or move in large numbers

uniform special set of clothes worn by a super hero

villain evil person

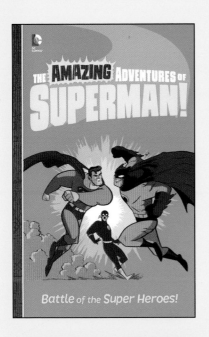

Battle of the Super Heroes!

Escape from Future World!

Alien Superman!

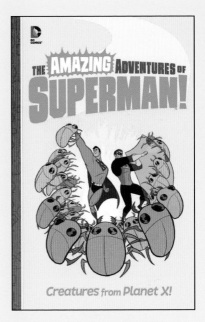

Creatures from Planet X!

COLLECT THEM ALL!

only from . . . RAINTREE